When God Run the Situation
A Death to Life Story

Leslie Simmons

Copyright © 2020 Leslie Simmons All rights reserved

The characters and events in this book are factual. Any similarity to other real persons, living or dead, is coincidental and not intended by the author.

No part of this book may be reproduced, or stored in a retrieval system, or transmitted in any form or by any means, electronic, mechanical, photocopying, recording, or otherwise, without express written permission of the publisher.

ISBN: 9798673078587
Independently published

Cover design by Melody James

DEDICATION

I dedicate this book to my little sister Aretha "Retha" Simmons, who inspired me to write this book.
It is because of you; I know hope, faith, and prayer will sometimes bring real miracles.
Love always, your big sister.

Contents

Introduction	1
A Walk to Remember	4
The First 48	9
Changing the Atmosphere	14
Speaking Life	18
Our Decision	22
The Final Decision	25
Anointed Oil	28
The Notebook	30
Living Off Prayer	37
The Shift	40
God Preparing to Run the Situation	42
Do Not Resuscitate	48
An Angel in Tennis Shoes	50
Against All Odds	54
Amazing Grace	63
From Death to Life	73

ACKNOWLEDGMENTS

To my children, Chandy, Dutchess, Melody, Melvin, and Tyra, without you all, I would have never known how to connect my emotions to words. To Aretha's neighbors, thank you for being her saving grace. To all my family and friends, that has encouraged me and all who took the time to visit, pray and speak profound words to lift Aretha's soul. To Aretha's care team: Doctors, nurses (past and present) who take care of my little sister. And to both of my parents, thank you for continuing to watch over me in spirit. Thank you all so much from the bottom of my heart! God chose you all to be in the "situation," and be a part of Aretha's incredible story!

My aunt has always said to me, "Lord Leslie, get to da point," and like always, I try not to leave out specific details, because you would not fully understand my story.

If you ever run into a situation where worry and fear seem to weigh you down, I pray this book will inspire you to trust and believe that a little faith is all you need to rise and allow God to run the situation.

Life does not choose you; you choose life!

INTRODUCTION

Mother's Day 2013, my sister Aretha spent the day with her three children, Kandice.

Mariah and Kalvon

When God Run the Situation

A Death to Life Story

Less than two weeks later, Aretha was at Carolina Medical Center, in Charlotte NC, on life support, fighting for her life!

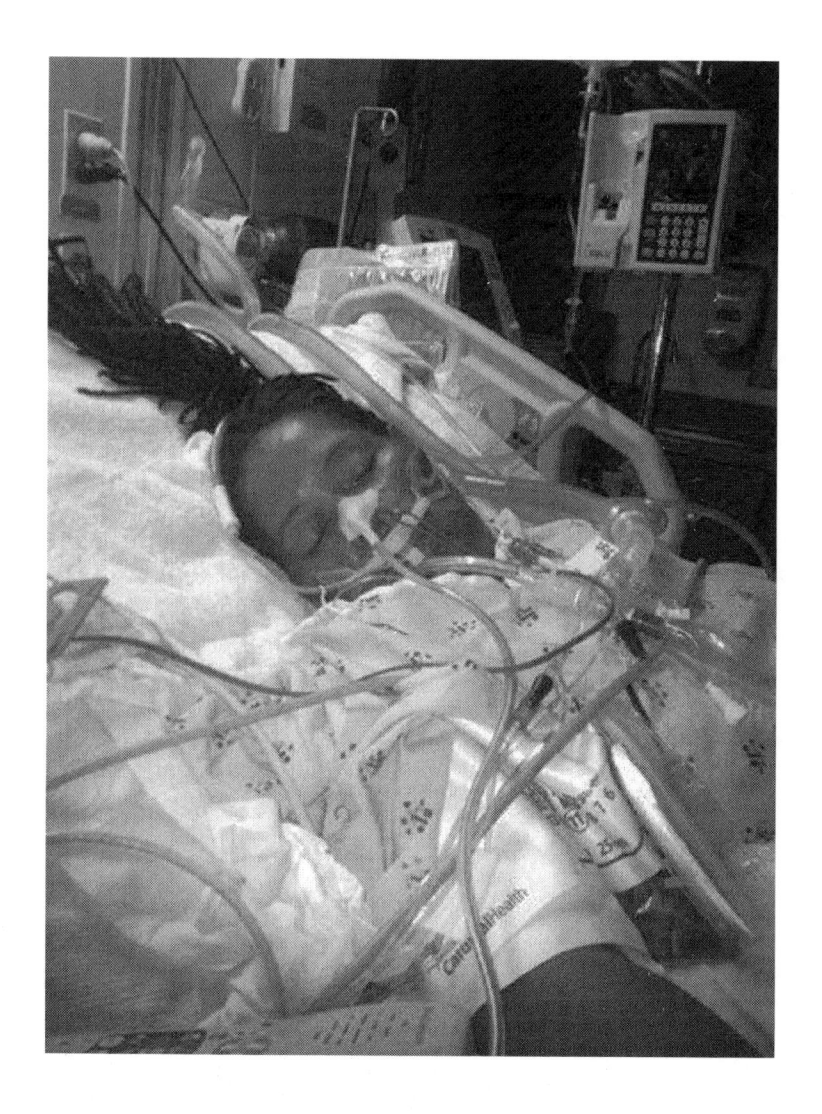

A Walk to Remember

A typical Friday morning for Aretha would usually mean watching her must-see tv shows: the first 48 and criminal minds. Her oldest daughter had gone to work, and her youngest daughter had already left out for school. Except for this morning, she went for a walk with her two-year-old son instead. Aretha's morning walk seemed to be going great! The fresh morning air, the neighborhood quiet and calm because everyone was gone to work. All, but one neighbor, running late for work.

When God Run the Situation

A Death to Life Story

A supervisor at the community hospice, usually punctual, noticed her husband had forgotten to take the trash to the curb, something he never fails to do. As she proceeded to take the trash to the curb, she heard, "help!" she noticed my nephew first, then Aretha, who had managed to make it back from her walk, laying on her porch, with her arm barely lifted in the air, calling for help!

Rushing to Aretha's aid, her neighbor called 911. Out of breath and losing consciousness Aretha was able to remember one number, her good friend, and another neighbor, who came to pick up my nephew and contacted other family members.

Aretha was rushed to the local hospital, in Rutherfordton, NC, and admitted into the Intensive Care Unit upon arrival.

When God Run the Situation
A Death to Life Story

On my way to Western Carolina University in Cullowhee, NC, I received a call from my aunt about Aretha. All I could hear her say was, "Aretha is in intensive care at Rutherford hospital." I listened to what she was saying, but at the same time, I could not process that thought! On the way back down the road, I had a nervous feeling in my gut. Aretha previously had three heart attacks, all of them which happen to be on a Friday. I knew this Friday; it was not going to be news of Aretha having another heart attack, like the other three. She would usually spend a few days in the hospital and back home to drink morning coffee with me, braid my hair, or dance to old school music. No! This feeling was different.

When I made it to the hospital, overwhelmed with fear, I went straight into the emergency room bathroom, where I sat in a stall, crying for about 20 minutes before my aunt called again to ask where I was? "Downstairs in the emergency room bathroom," I replied. My aunt came down to get me; I continued to cry. I could not prepare myself to see my little sister, "She's in critical condition." I kept thinking. My aunt came down to get me, with her hands wrapped around me, she said, "Are you ready now? Because your sister needs you!"

When God Run the Situation

A Death to Life Story

The First 48

On the way up to ICU, I still had a knot in my stomach; I could barely breathe because I did not know what to expect. Walking into the room, I knew, at that moment, my gut feeling was right. My sister had all these tubes hooked up to her to help her breathe. Yes! She was in critical condition. Considering Aretha's medical condition and previous heart attacks, the facility in Rutherfordton, NC, felt she needed to be moved to a bigger facility an hour away in Charlotte, NC, right away! While we waited on the helicopter to airlift Aretha to Charlotte, I did not think twice about whether I was going or not. I knew, even with my heavy responsibilities: work, home, kids, and a relationship; I had to be there by my little sister's side.

Leslie Simmons

All I could think about is the picture Aretha had sent me on Mother's Day and how pretty she looked.

When God Run the Situation

A Death to Life Story

When I made it to Carolina Medical Center, several friends and family members had already heard the news of Aretha's condition and was genuinely concerned. Many were en route or had already made it to Charlotte, to give a hand, support, and hugs.

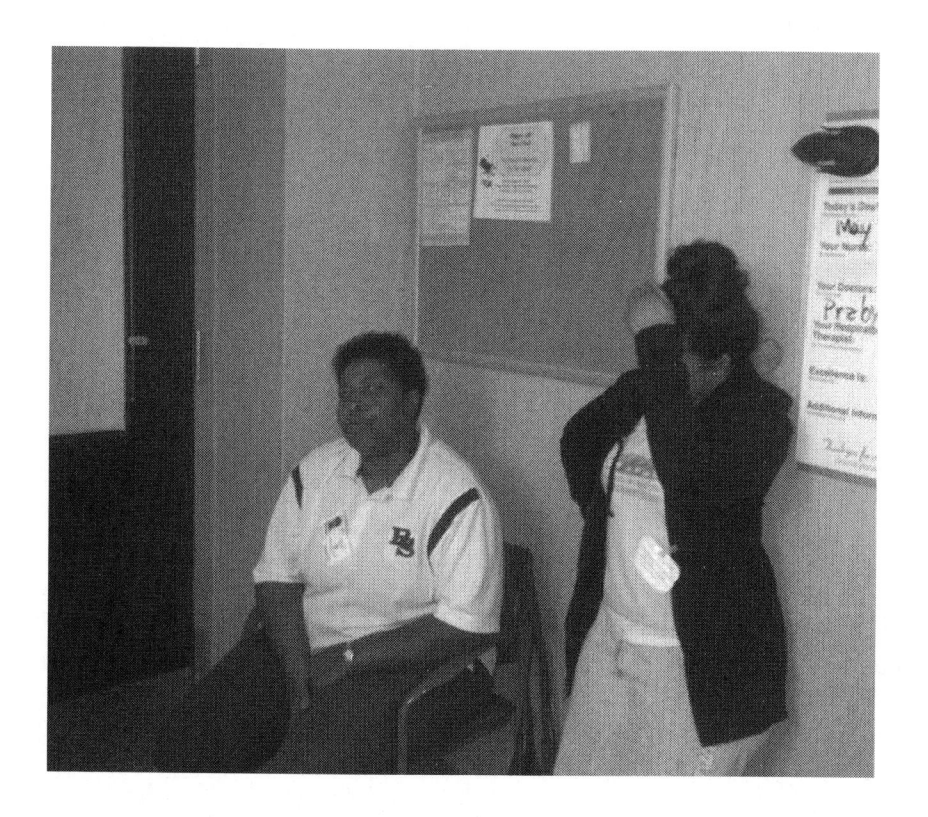

Once Aretha got settled in her room, I sat down by her side, waiting to hear her say something! Seem like days went by before her doctor entered the room to read the diagnosis; A diagnosis we were not prepared to hear! She had lost too much oxygen to her brain from blood clots and had gone into a coma. She was officially brain dead. "A coma... brain dead... No!"
"She's going to wake up and say something!" "Maybe the doctors were all wrong!"'...Breathe," I kept telling myself. "She knows her big sister is here." " The First 48 is on; she's going to wake up!"

Before I knew it, a week had passed, and Aretha's conditions had not changed.

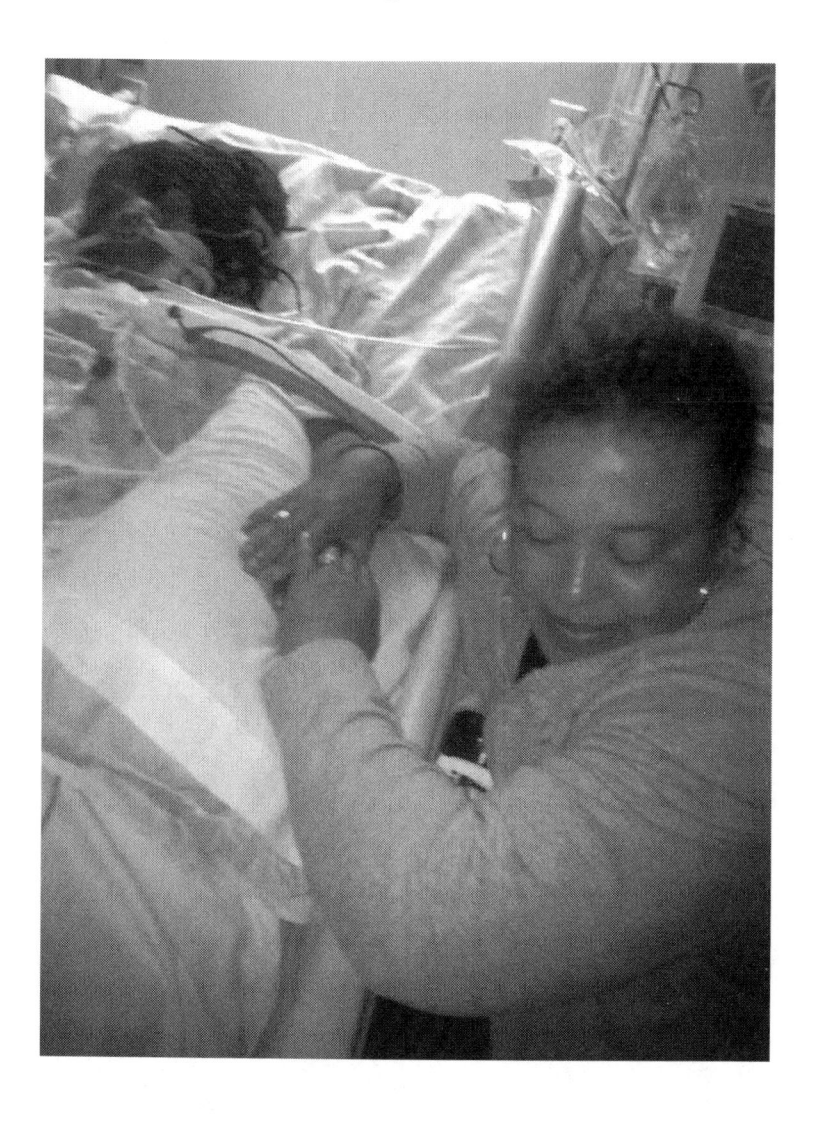

Changing the Atmosphere

While at the Carolina medical center in Charlotte, NC, Aretha had many family and friends visiting her daily. For weeks, several family members never left her side. Some even camped out.

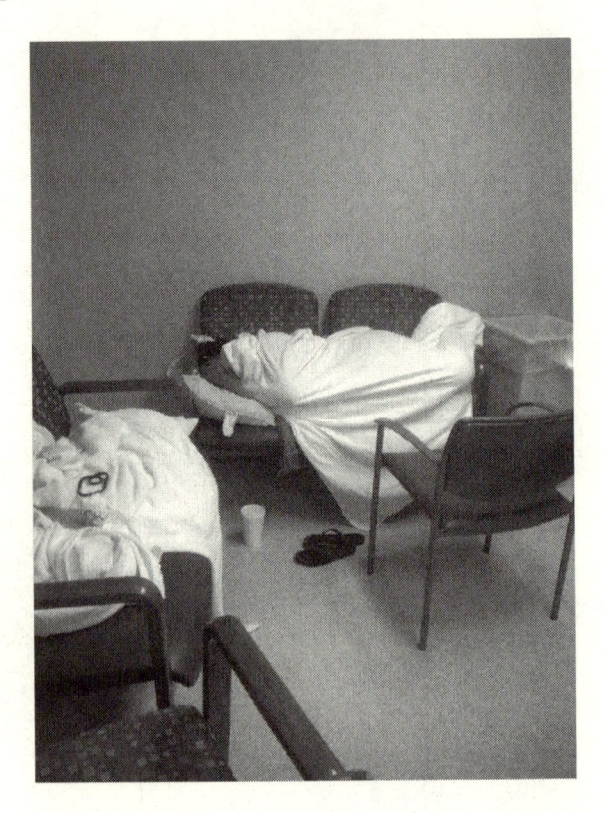

Other family members made sure that no one went without food, a shower, and had money in their pockets. My aunt made sure we kept a positive attitude in a negative situation. "change the atmosphere," She said. Preachers also called, visited, confirmed the same thing, "Change the atmosphere and listen for God's word."

One day, our county's reverend came to visit when he came into Aretha's room, looked at Aretha, turned, and right back out! There were too many people standing in her room, talking, along with the tv on. He said, "The atmosphere is so important." Confirmation!" We followed his instructions and began changing the atmosphere and limited people in her room.

When God Run the Situation

A Death to Life Story

It just so happens that Carolina Medical Center had newly installed a new computer system. "Yes! The internet!" I thought pandora has excellent stations to calm the atmosphere.

Speaking Life

Over ten doctors were caring for Aretha. Every morning the doctor on call would check her vitals. I knew it was not right, but before the doctor could get a word out, I would say, "Can we step outside the room please!" (more Godly counsel) came from our aunt. She said, "don't let them doctors speak death; if they are not speaking life, asked them nicely to step outside the room, " The doctor's response to Aretha's vitals daily was, "She's not responding, I'm sorry!" Aretha was still on life support, and on 100% oxygen after a week and a half, she could not breathe independently. The doctors caring for her felt that there was nothing else medically that they could do.

The family would have to decide to leave her on or take her off life support. The Cardiologist and another doctor on call explained that "her heart was weak, and her vitals were still not good." They all agreed that keeping Aretha on life support was not saving her life, only prolonging it.

We were down to one option, one hope! To see if Aretha had any brain activity! I believed the neurologist report would be the answer to everything! Waiting on his medical information and his medical point of view had my hopes too high! Waiting seemed like an eternity. We were all anxious for the neurologist report because he could tell us more and explain Aretha's brain activity better!

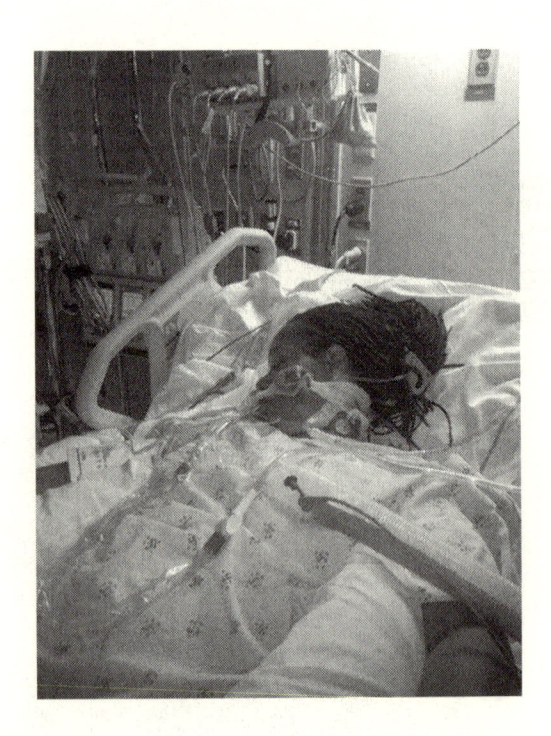

The neurologist took a few days to get back with us. The morning he came in, he checked Aretha's vitals. I asked him if we could step outside the room, he said: "I know that the family was waiting on my report, and I hate to be the barrier of bad news and remove the little hope your family has for Ms. Aretha, but she does not have any brain activity, at all; there has been too much damage from the lack of oxygen to her brain, that all four lobes are damaged, and the damage was not irreversible, the state she is in now, will be her state for the rest of her life." My heart dropped, and I felt my body physically shaking.

Our Decision

The news that Aretha would be a vegetable (mentally disable) the rest of her life was devastating! The doctors came to us once again to ask," Have the Family decided on removing Ms. Aretha from life support?" There will be a time in your life when you will have no choice but to call on God! If you do not know how to pray or have a relationship with him, you better get Someone else you know without a doubt that will teach you how! I called my aunt first.

All I could think about was the love I know my sister had for her three kids and the love I had for her. I called my aunt, with tears running down my face, and said, "We don't want to take Aretha off life support!

When God Run the Situation

A Death to Life Story

We cannot make that decision; we cannot! She hasn't heard her son's first words!" I told my aunt, "I don't want to seem selfish, but if God would spare my sister's life, I will accept her in that state!" I went on talking, that's when said, "Hush for a minute, Leslie, so I can understand what you are saying! Then she said, "Alright, tell the Doctors!" The family decision is final; we want to keep her on life support!

My brother, nieces, and I sat down with the doctors and found out our decision to keep Aretha on life support may not be an option. Over ten doctor's medical opinions about Aretha were she "medically brain dead."

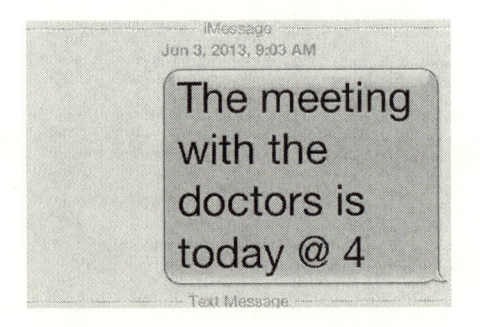

> The meeting with the doctors is today @ 4

There was nothing medically they could do to save her life because of all her health problems. We still stood our ground with keeping her on life support. After a few days, our decision went to the ethics board, which had me anxious. A new doctor, nurse, social worker, case manager, and a priest. Had the power to override our decisions.

When God Run the Situation

A Death to Life Story

Final Decision

The meeting with the ethics board members did not go well! But I knew that Aretha had people praying for her from the Queen city to the city of Brotherly love! Saints and sinners were praying, calling, and visiting. As we expected, the decision was final! The doctor, who was also the head of the ethics board, described Aretha's condition with this scenario, "A kitten can be in the middle of a river, hanging on a tree branch, out of danger, but with nowhere to jump, he would still be in trouble!" Aretha had too many medical problems working against her health to believe treating one of her health issues would adjust the rest. (she would still be in danger!) Aretha was coming off life support, and there was nothing we could do.

The doctor said, "Sorry!" There was nothing medically; at this point, they could do. Yes! The decision was final!

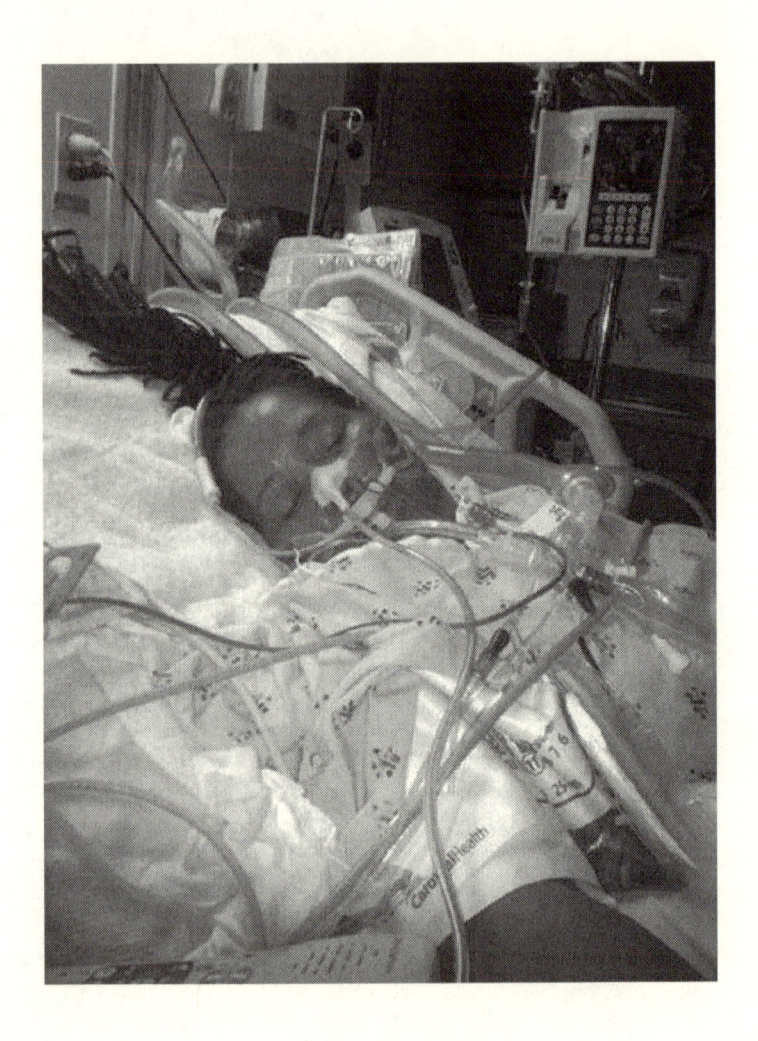

When God Run the Situation

A Death to Life Story

The head of the ethics board told us he was going out of town for an early Father's Day getaway and would be back the following Monday; he gave us his cell phone number and said, "I'm sorry! If there are any questions, call me; God Bless!" We had just a few days to say our goodbyes!

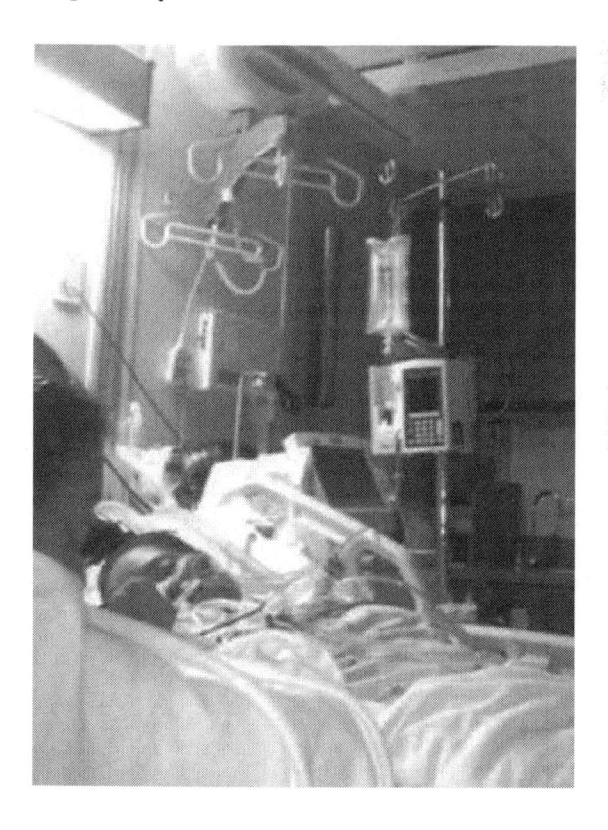

Anointed Oil

After the ethics board meeting, our aunt came to visit Aretha, she always prayed for Aretha before she left, but this time, she said, "I wish I had some oil. I said, "I can go look in my car; I would not be surprised if some oil is in there. She said, " Go look, Leslie!". Well, guess what? I found a brand-new bottle of Johnson baby oil! On my way back up to Aretha's room, I was "shaking" and saying to myself, "Wow! This is not luck!" Our aunt prayed over that oil, anointed the doors, bed, and the equipment that kept Aretha alive; She put oil in Aretha's head. She said, "do this every time you think about it, "... and I did!

I would put the anointed oil on the doors, oxygen machine, and Aretha's head throughout the day.

The doctors were still coming by every morning to do their assessment. Aretha was still "unresponsive," but something unique happened! Her eyes had opened, but they had set! To me, it was a response; I did not post anything on social media! Instead, I texted everyone with the good news that I knew would be as happy as I was about Aretha opening her eyes.

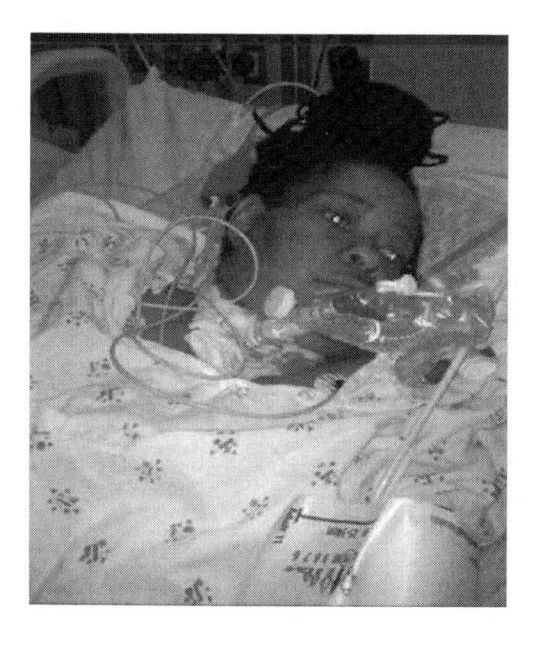

Notebook

I was excited! But I still felt like my life was about to end as well, not my little sister! The feeling was surreal!

One night, while listening to gospel on pandora, in Aretha's room.

"Healing" by Richard Smallwood.

"Broken, But I'm Healed" by Lucinda Moore.

"It Ain't Over" by Maurette Brown Clark

"Be Still "by Yolanda Adams, and "Praise Him in Advance" by Marvin Sapp came on in that order.

The next morning, while watching tv, Pastor Joel Osteen said, "God won't wait on a committee; he will pressure whoever until he gets what he wants!"

My racing thoughts were, "God, the ethics board has decided to override our decision on keeping Aretha on life support; over ten doctors agreed!

The neurologist stated, "No brain activity!"... But GOD!!

I had all these thoughts running through my mind, and so many unexpected blessings were happening that my mind started to race even more. I explained this to my aunt; she said, "Start writing everything down!"

When God Run the Situation

A Death to Life Story

My cousin, a principal in Charlotte, NC, wanted to get me pens, pencils, and paper over to Carolina medical center right away. The teachers were happy to give what they had handy; pens, markers, stickers, and this one notebook that just so happen to be red!

I started writing everything in the red notebook, not to

forget words, gestures, and blessings. I even noted

updates from the doctors.

One day the neurologist stopped by, doing his morning assessment; Aretha's eyes were still open "set" she had started yawning too. I was excited because she had never done this before! He stated, "The lack of oxygen had severely damaged Aretha's brain lobes."

Her body was (posturing), which was not any signs of improvement. The yawing was a normal reaction.

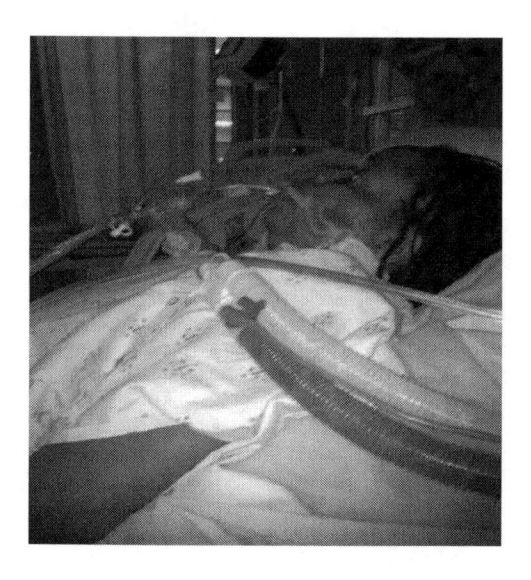

I remember talking to one of my cousins with hope and sadness simultaneously; I told her about how I only had a day or two left to spend with my little sister and how I felt like Aretha was trying to tell me something! She said, "God is working on changing the medical decision and a new set of doctors." I believed those words with all my heart!

Living Off Prayers

Prayers were still going up! Aretha still had many friends and family calling and visiting to say their goodbyes. I used the anointed oil, changed the atmosphere, and even limited the number of people in her room; The only sign of life to the family was her eyes were open, and she was yawning! But all of this was medically normal! I could not come to terms with saying goodbye!

My unselfish prayer for my little sister's life was "God if Aretha had a million-dollar life insurance policy with me as the beneficiary. I still would keep her on life support, please; for me, I'm not ready my sister to leave me!"

With prayer and prayers of others, I was able to stay focused. My aunt said, "my ears are against God's lips, and he's telling me, it's okay!"

"Still listen for the word of God."

"Aretha is going to be a testimony!"

"God is working on my cousin's brain."

"God ain't done yet, Leslie! Dry your tears and dry them now!" "keep listening for the word of God!"

"God will change the reports and the doctors."

When God Run the Situation

A Death to Life Story

I kept praying to "God, please do what you do best, if those doctors had their glasses on, please allow them to take them off, if their glasses were off, please allow them to put them on, please for me, because my sister has never heard her son's first words." People have always said, "What would Aretha do without you, Leslie?" Now I wondered what I would do without her.

The Shift

The next morning, I had awakened to see a new doctor I had not seen before. He did his assessment and said, "Do Ms. Simmons have children?" I said, "Yes!" He stood there looking at Aretha, then he looked at me and said, "God bless! If you have any questions, let me know!" After the new doctor left, the neurologist came in with the same news, like before, he does not see any improvement! But this time, he paused and said, "But we are not God!" I responded, "WHAT?! I could not believe what I was hearing! I said, "THAT'S ALL I NEEDED TO HEAR! So this is all Science! Even you cannot be 100% sure what is going on in her brain!" JUST SCIENCE!

When God Run the Situation

A Death to Life Story

Aretha had opened her eyes fuller, and certain things we would be saying around would cause her blood pressure to go up; when she saw her kids, her blood pressure would change. I knew she was saying, "Please don't give up on me, sister!" and I did not!

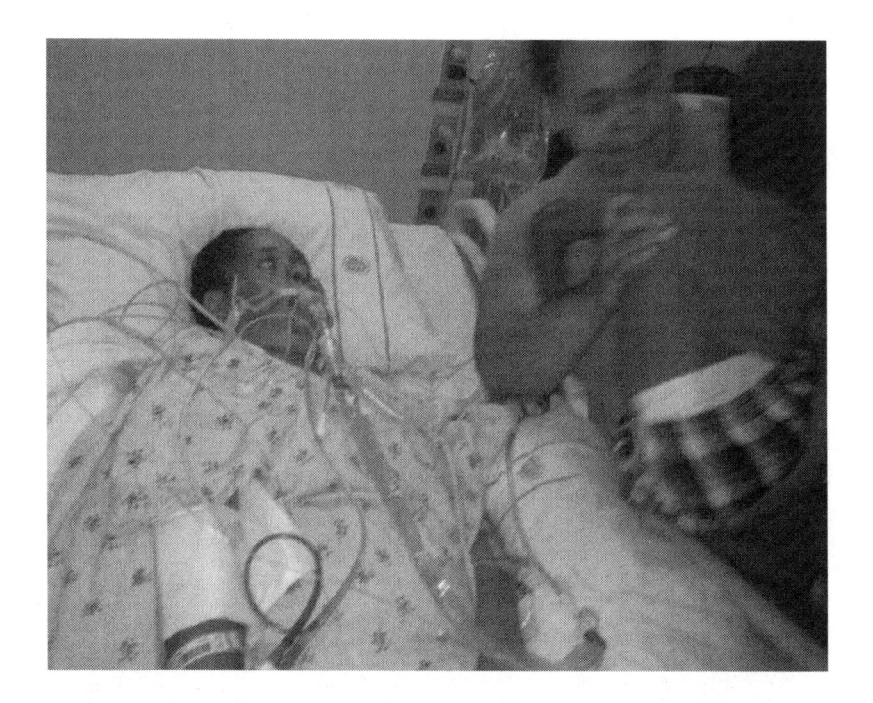

God Preparing To Run The Situation

My niece Mariah and I were sitting in the hallway of the hospital. I noticed my niece was watching these two ladies, walking toward us, one with long blonde hair, dressed in a tee-shirt, old cut-off jean shorts, and these new tennis shoes. When they got close, my niece said, "Excuse me, ma'am, have you been digging in my mom's closet? Because she is the only one who has tennis shoes like those! "Smiling, the lady and her friend stopped to talk to us. She started witnessing and told us about her mom, who had a heart attack and was in ICU. I said, "Yes! Across from my sister, I thought I recognized you two." I had seen them in a room, across from Aretha, earlier.

When God Run the Situation

A Death to Life Story

After talking to her for a few minutes, we found out; she had gone through the same medical situation Aretha was going through. She had been in a coma and was sent home with a trachea, to die; She stated Her husband had left her for the caregiver because she was dead, to him. She talked about how she heard everything while in a coma; and to stay mindful that even though Aretha was in a coma, she could still hear everything spoken! She asked if she could meet and pray for Aretha! We were delighted and excited to give her the opportunity for some reason.

Detoured already; she wanted to meet Aretha. We all walked back to the intensive care unit, Laughing and talking, like old friends.

When she walked into Aretha's room, she kissed her on the forehead and said, "I love you!" She whispered something in Aretha's ear and rubbed her leg, for the first time in weeks, Aretha raised her legs! We all started screaming, jumping, and hollering with amazement; We all had tears of joy rolling down our cheeks!

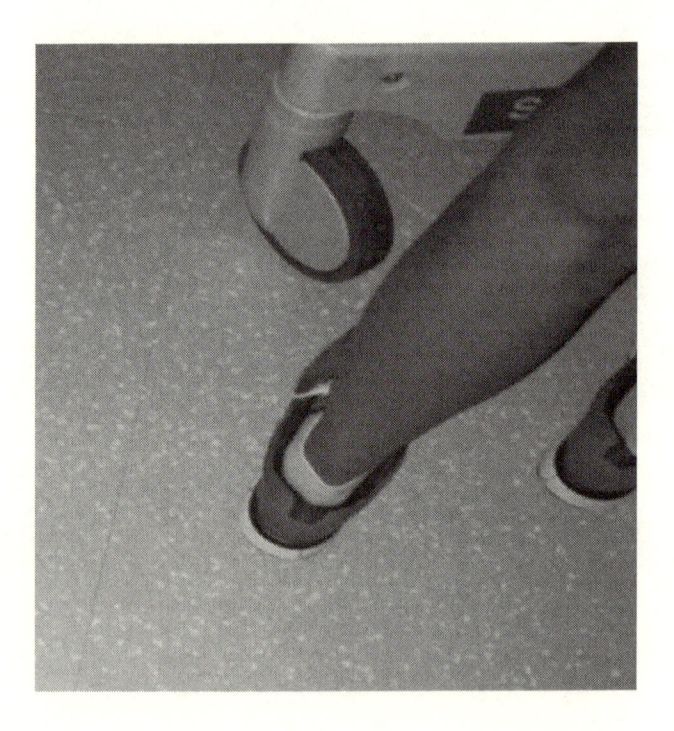

When God Run the Situation
A Death to Life Story

Like always, I started snapping photos to capture this incredible moment! She prayed, rubbed, and kissed on Aretha as though she knew her. After she whispered something else in Aretha's ear, she said, "I hate to leave! But I must go!"

On her way out the door, she hugged and kissed all of us and kept saying, "I love all of you, I love you all!". I asked her for her name and number when she was on her way out the door, but she and her friend acted like they did not want me to have it. While ignoring my request, she stood in the doorway and repeated, "I love all of you; I love you all!" I did not get her name or number. Remembering, her mom was in ICU, across from Aretha. I figured I would see her again to update her on Aretha's medical condition if there were any changes.

I told our aunt about how Aretha was moving when the lady visited her, and how the tennis shoes sparked our meeting! I also shared this one photo of her rough-looking hand rubbing across Aretha's leg (That mysteriously disappeared). Our aunt's response was, "That looks like the hand of God!"

Our aunt paused and said, "I want Someone to get Aretha's tennis shoes and put them under her bed! Also, put the Bible scripture **John 5:8 KJV "Jesus saith unto him, Rise, take up thy bed, and walk."** on her bed,

Then she asked me if I knew where the prayer shaw was she had given me two years earlier while visiting Pastor Joel Osteen church in Texas. When my aunt put the prayer shaw around me, she told me I would need it in the future! The future was now! She said, "Lay that prayer shaw, over Aretha's body."

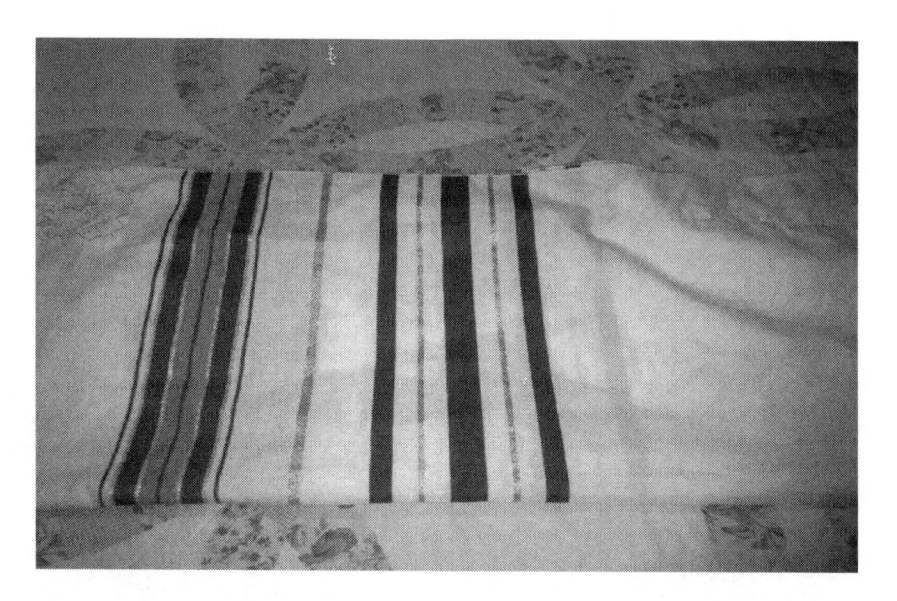

Do Not Resuscitate

Aretha's had started moving so much; we knew it had to be more than posturing! So, we took our chance with the "New" doctor to see if there was anything else medically possible to save Aretha's life. We went to him, to my surprise, the new doctor suggested a trachea. Yes! A trachea, with the advice from one of the previous doctors that to do the trachea, the family would have to sign a DNR "do not resuscitate," which means while in surgery, if she went into cardiac arrest, they would not revive her! Aretha was in a coma state with a weak heart! The Cardiologist said she would not pull through this type of surgery!

Aretha was moving more, and continuously the nurses had to put a mitten on her hand to keep her from pulling her tubes out.

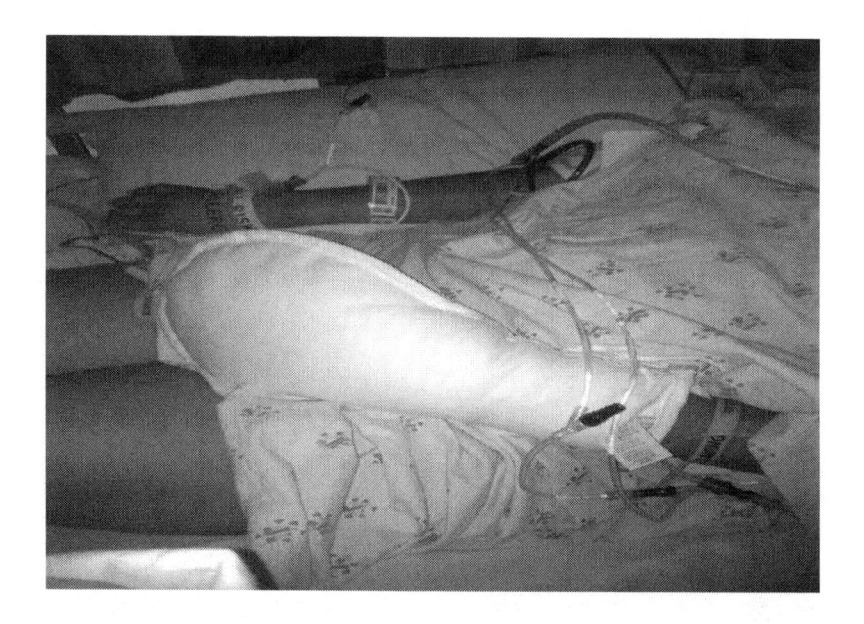

An Angel In Tennis Shoes

My cousin, her husband, and their son came over to bring us a hot meal and to have prayer for Aretha's trachea surgery. My cousin's husband, who is also a pastor, said, "I heard about the lady with the new tennis shoes that came by to pray for Aretha's! Then he went on to say he had mentioned it to his mom! With a smile, he said, "My God! Leslie, my mom told me to tell you, you all will never see that woman again! I said, "Yes, we will, she's across the hall with her mom!" We both looked over at the other rooms, still smiling and shaking his head. "My God!" He said, "My God!"

All the rooms were empty!

When God Run the Situation

A Death to Life Story

I physically started to shake! Puzzled and confused, I went over to the nursing station in the middle of the ICU rooms; I asked the nurse, "Where was the older lady in the room and if they had moved her?" I went on to say, "Her daughter and a friend were over there with her, a few days go! I believe she had a heart attack!" The nurse said, "No one has been in these rooms for over a week!" I could not speak! But I still had all the photos of the lady rubbing and kissing Aretha. To my SURPRISE!!

All the photos I took! I only captured her back, hand, and tennis shoes.

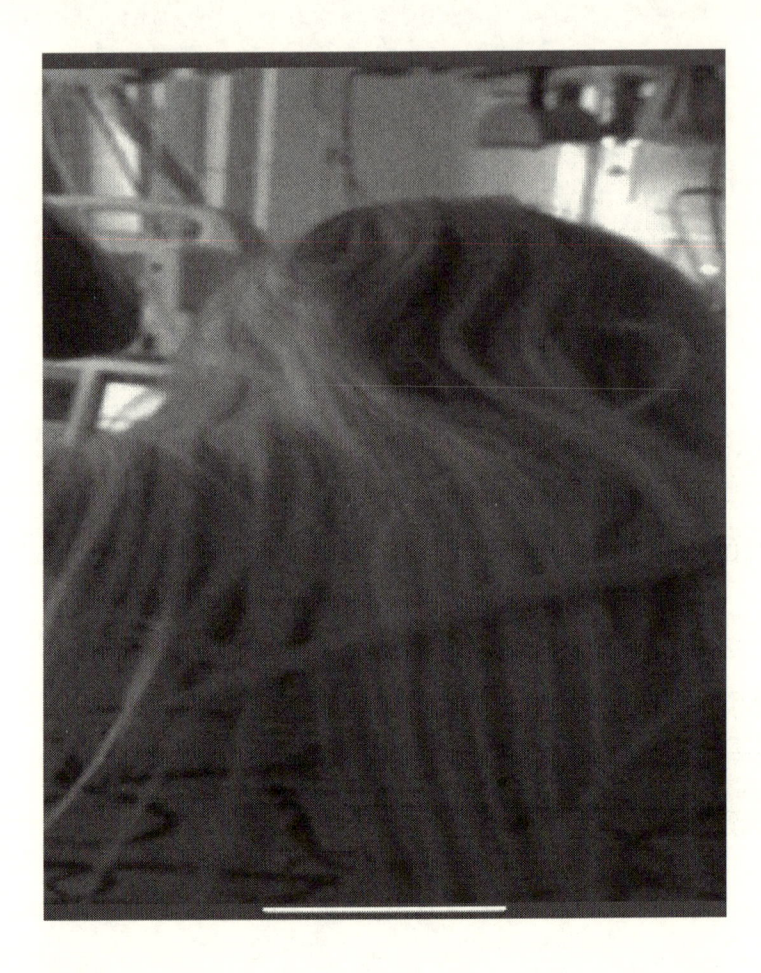

When God Run the Situation

A Death to Life Story

All I could say, with tears running down my face, was, Thank you! Thank you! God! For sending my mom, who had died from a massive heart attack in Aretha's bedroom almost 17 years earlier, "Thank you!" I believe God had sent our mom, Aretha's guardian angel, wearing those tennis shoes, just like Aretha had, to whisper in her ear, "Aretha, I love you, this is Ardell, don't you give up! I knew God had intervened and had taken over! God himself was running the situation;

A calm, relaxed emotion came over my mind and body. My little sister, I felt, was going to be okay!

Against All Odds

When the doctor, the head of the ethics board,

returned from his Father's Day getaway, he was

astonished by Aretha's progress.

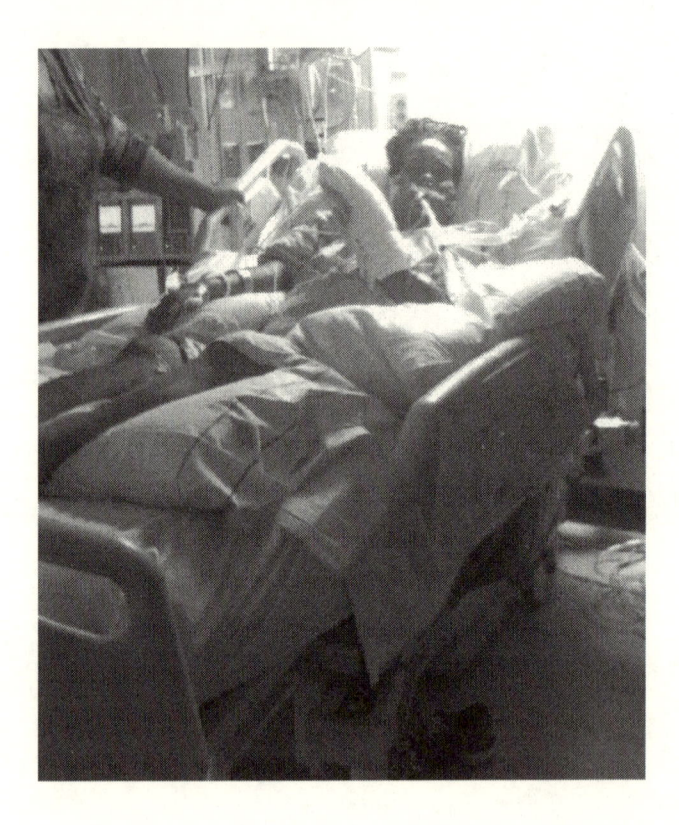

After reviewing Aretha's miraculous progress, he and the other board members agreed with the new doctor to try the trachea surgery with the DNR in place. With a 5% survival rate, the odds stacked against Aretha. WE SIGNED THE DNR!!

Leslie Simmons

When Aretha went into surgery, we all were at peace.

In Charlotte, NC, we decided to go to the boardwalk to

relax our bodies and minds.

When God Run the Situation

A Death to Life Story

It was knowing that God was running the 95% death situation back at Carolina Medical Center. We were able to smile for the time in weeks, even if it was just a half one.

Leslie Simmons

Aretha came out of surgery without any complications.

We were so grateful God spared Aretha's life!

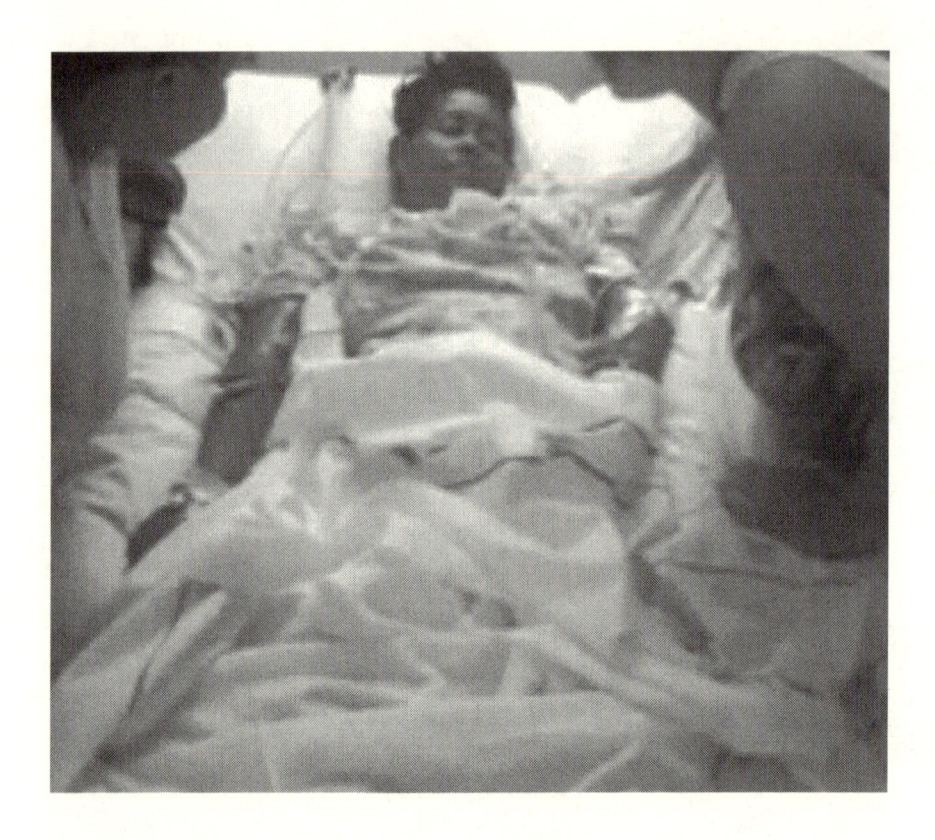

The on-call nurse read her bracelet, "A life worth saving," a bracelet, one our cousins had put on her wrist; her nurse said, "Yes, you are lady, you are a miracle!!

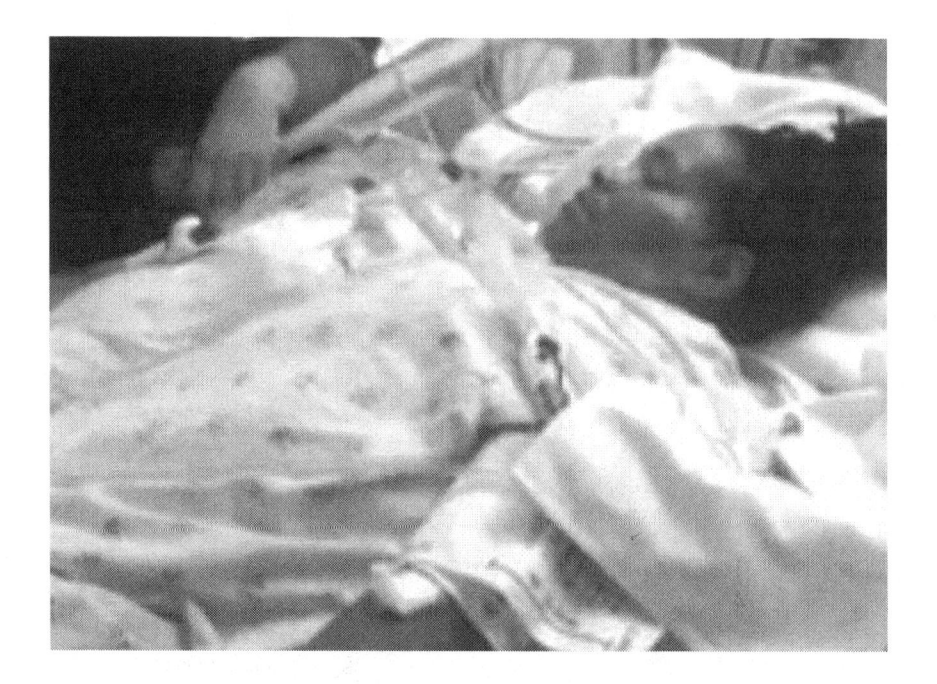

The trachea was a success, Aretha was now off life support, breathing own her own, and her eyes seemed fuller. She had not realized the stress her body went through, but I could see it physically on her face

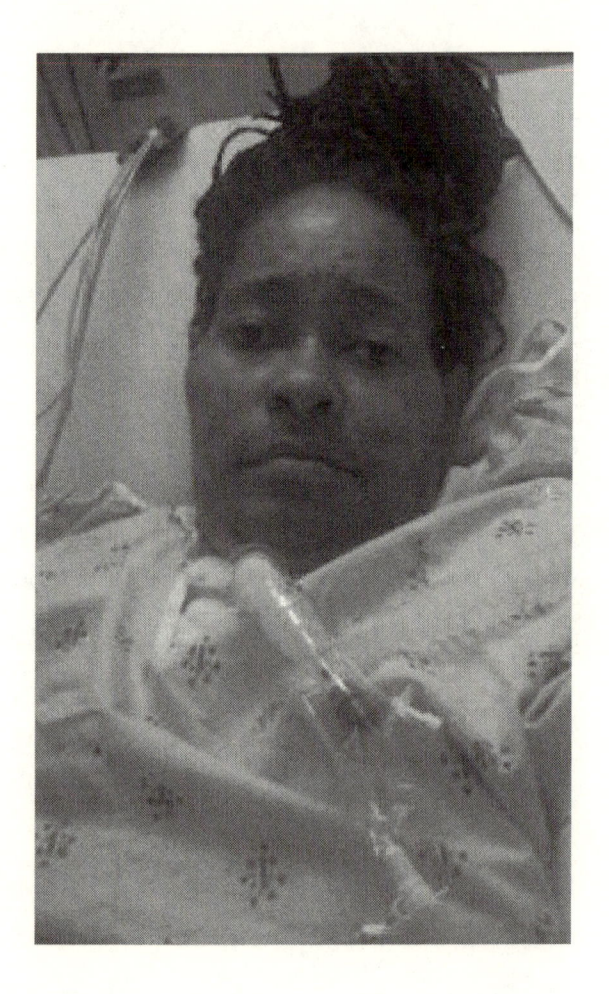

A few days after Aretha's successful trachea surgery, she moved to the progressive floor. We continued to monitor visits, pour oil in her head, post the bible scripture **John 5:8 KJV, "Jesus saith unto him, "Rise, take up thy bed, and walk."** and kept the atmosphere peaceful with praise music!

Family and friends were so happy Aretha had progressed so well, everyone was overwhelmed with joy, God spared Aretha's life.

Aretha could respond to yes or no questions by shaking her head; her family and friends would drive an hour to talk and laugh with her for just ten minutes. One of her friends would always ask her, "Are you ready to go to Dollywood?" A place where Aretha would say she was taking her kids before her "Miracle" She always would shake her head yes, extremely fast. We all were happy with any small gesture. I would never have imagined that a swift yes or no nod would fill my day with much joy, laughter, and hope.

When God Run the Situation

A Death to Life Story

Amazing Grace

Aretha was progressing so well; she even surprised the nurses and doctors. She began communicating with us by mouth (no sound) with her trachea in place, we had to read her lips, but we could understand her clearly! I knew God was restoring Aretha's brain completely when she looked at her daughter with a concerned look and said, with no voice," Where's my pocketbook and my food stamp card?" My niece laughed with tears in her eyes. Aretha did not realize she had been in the hospital for over a month, and she knew nothing about her near-death situation. The time Aretha spent in the hospital, my son, her nephew, had grown a few inches, and his voice had changed.

The day he walked in Aretha's room, she looked at him for a minute with this confused look, moving her lips, she said, "Is that Melvin?" We started hollering, laughing, and crying once again with joy!

Yes! My little sister's memory was restoring.

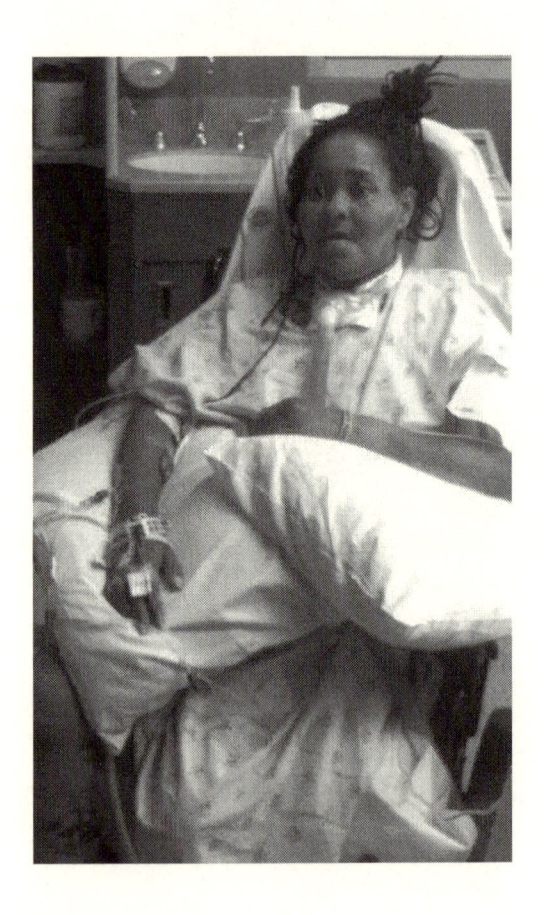

After the trachea surgery, Aretha continued to progress so well; the doctors transferred her to Peaks Resource in Shelby, NC, for rehabilitation.

The bible scripture **John 5:8 KJV, "Jesus saith unto him, "Rise, take up thy bed, and walk."** was no longer taped to her bed, the first 48 was back on, and no praise music played in the background! We all went back to our daily lives.

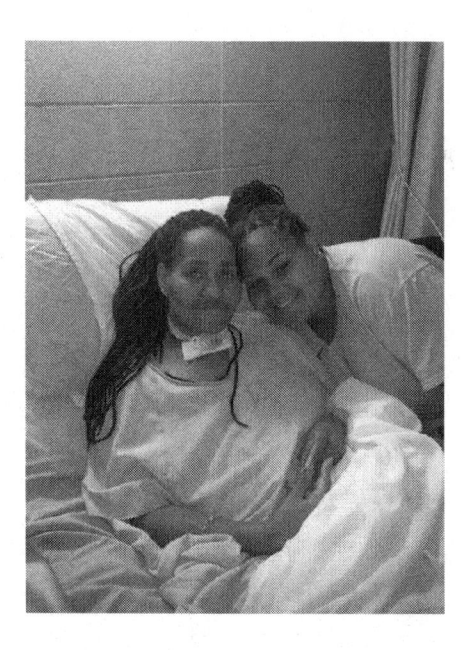

GOD HAD A WAY OF GETTING OUR ATTENTION ONCE AGAIN!

When God Run the Situation

A Death to Life Story

Aretha went from fighting for her life to fighting with her kids once again.

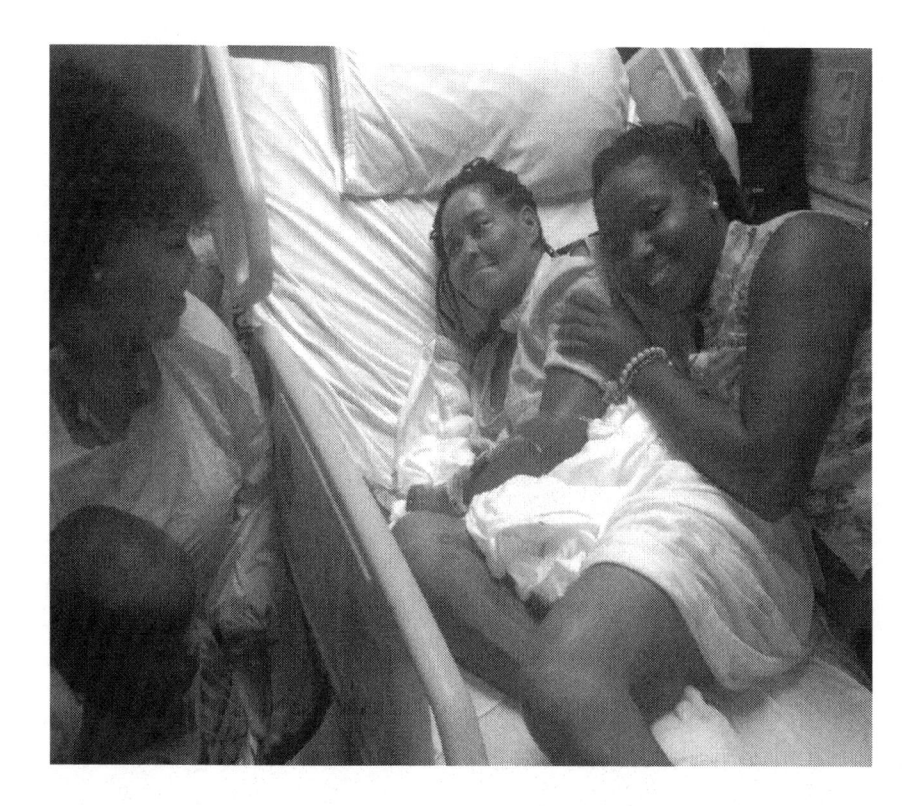

After a week at Peaks Resources, Aretha had to be readmitted back into the hospital, in Shelby, NC. Her right leg and foot were showing signs of discoloration.

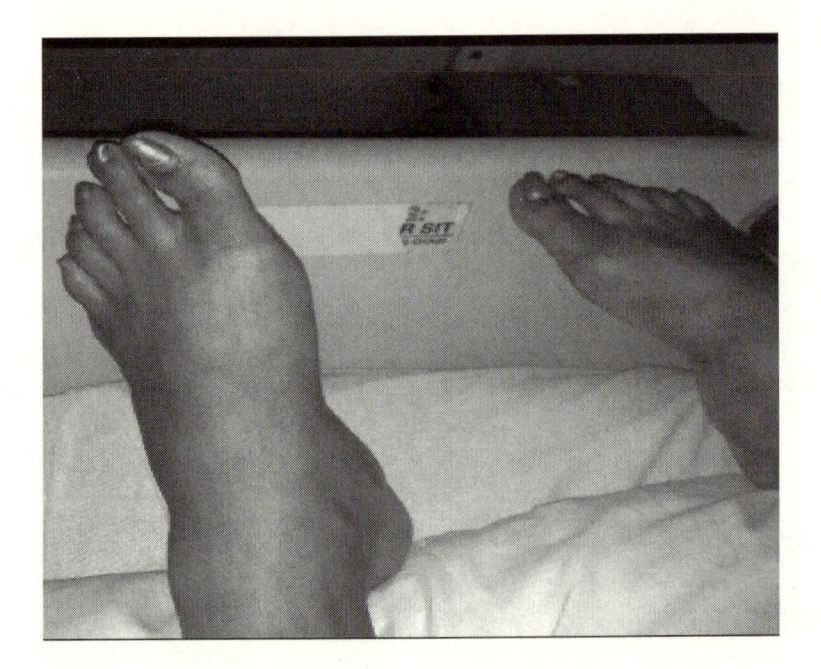

When God Run the Situation

A Death to Life Story

The doctors came to the family, again, with more bad news. Aretha's right leg had lost all circulation due to blood clots. She was diffidently going to lose her leg; amputation was the only option. Everybody that knows Aretha knows she has always had beautiful legs, feet, and hands. Her legs are so muscular; people thought she played sports or ran track; I would tell people that "Aretha never even played kickball!"

The family had to meet with the doctor to discuss the surgery and the possible outcome. Before the operation, another DNR would have to be signed. The doctor discussed his concerns, and this type of surgery was very severe, and he was afraid, after looking at Aretha's chart, that there was a 95% chance she would not pull through the surgery. The doctor said, "Someone had mentioned Ms. Simmons had a two-year-old son. He paused and said, "She's so young, I'm sorry! God bless!" If there are any questions, let me know!" At that moment, I knew God was going to run the 5% survival situation in the operating room at Cleveland Memorial Hospital. Once again! WE SIGNED THE DNR!!

Aretha went into her first surgery, with a 5% survival chance.

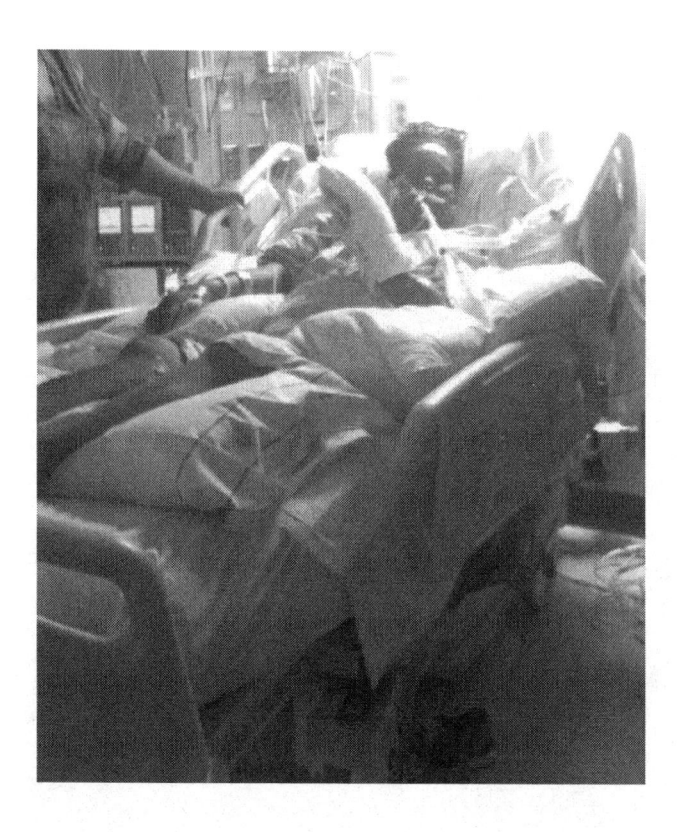

Aretha went into a second major surgery, with 95% no survival chance. Before both of the major surgeries, we signed the DNR; both times, she came out without complications.

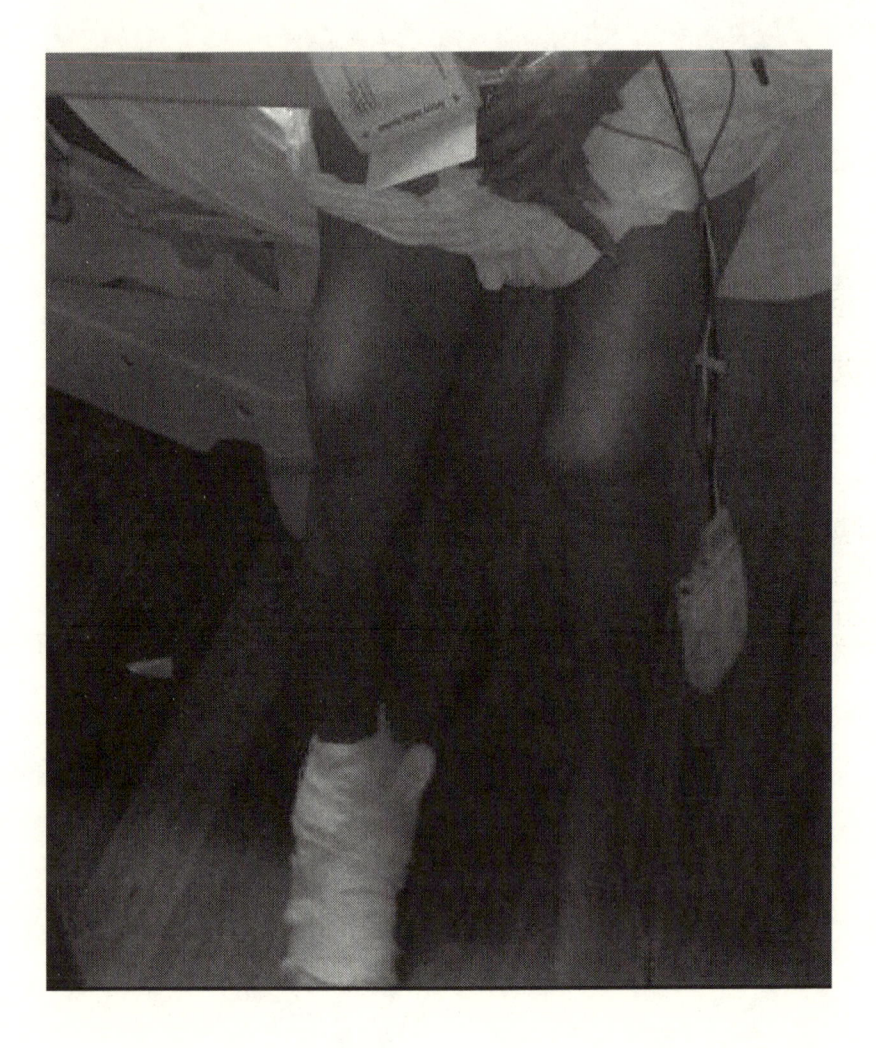

When God Run the Situation

A Death to Life Story

From Death To Life

Through Aretha's miraculous death to life story, being with my little sister was the most incredible experience I have ever witnessed.

A doctor explained to us; when Aretha stopped taking her blood thinner, blood clots formed, traveling to her heart (like shaking a cloth with small flying dust particles)

Aretha's pumping heart sent many blood clots through her body, many clots went to her brain, and many clots went to her leg.

Thank God for running the situation, because Aretha lost her leg and didn't lose her mind!

I can not begin to explain the events, people, and timing that took place in 2013. I can only attempt to explain how it feels to be giving a time stamp on a loved one's life.

Aretha had over 200 visits and calls, some for prayer and some to say their goodbyes! Without any knowledge of her situation. To this day, she still does not know and fully understands how close she came to death.

I can only give God all the glory for reversing decisions, reversing the blood clots, reversing the survival percentages, and, most of all, for running the situations to allow the events, people, and timing to change Aretha's story.

When God Run the Situation

A Death to Life Story

A Death

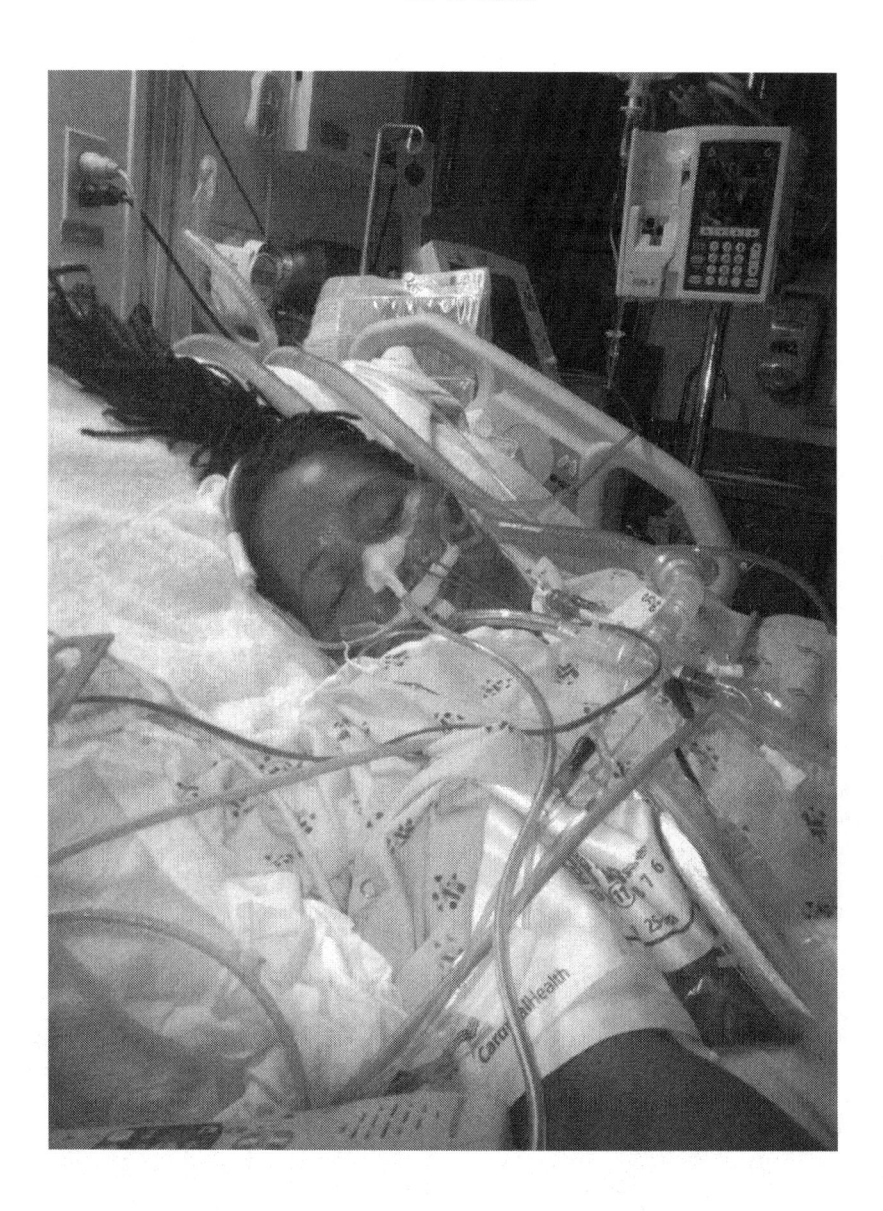

Leslie Simmons

To Life Story

When God Run the Situation

A Death to Life Story

JOHN 5:8, KJV: JESUS SAITH UNTO HIM, "RISE, TAKE UP THY BED, AND WALK."

Leslie Simmons

Aretha Today, 2020

When God Run the Situation

A Death to Life Story

Made in the USA
Columbia, SC
13 October 2020